Dirty Bertie

YUCK!

For Sarah and Paul – I haven't danced to
Culture Club since 1984! ~ D R
For the fab Frosties ~ A M

STRIPES PUBLISHING
An imprint of Little Tiger Press
1 The Coda Centre, 189 Munster Road,
London SW6 6AW

A paperback original
First published in Great Britain in 2008

Characters created by David Roberts
Text copyright © Alan MacDonald, 2008
Illustrations copyright © David Roberts, 2008

ISBN: 978-1-84715-039-4

Printed and bound in the UK.

10 9 8

Dirty Bertie

YUCK!

DAVID ROBERTS WRITTEN BY ALAN MACDONALD

Stripes

Collect all the
Dirty Bertie books!

Contents

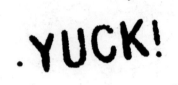

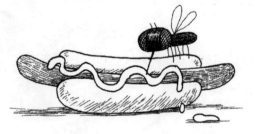

CHAPTER 1

Bertie dumped his bag and coat in the hall and burst into the kitchen. His mum was writing a letter.

"Mum! Guess what?"

"Hello, Bertie!" said Mum. "How was school?"

"Oh, the same," said Bertie. "But Mum, you'll never guess what…"

Dirty Bertie

"Probably not," said Mum, going back to her letter.

"There's a fair tomorrow night!" cried Bertie, excitedly. He waited for his mum to jump up and turn cartwheels. But she just said "Mmm" and went on writing.

"A funfair, Mum, with rides and prizes and everything!"

"Yes, you said."

"So can I go? Tomorrow night. Please Mum, can I?" Bertie was hopping from foot to foot as if he needed the toilet.

Mum looked up. "No, Bertie. I don't think so."

Bertie's mouth dropped open. "But … but why not?"

"Because I said so. I took you to the funfair last year and I remember what happened."

Dirty Bertie

Bertie cast his mind back
to last year. True, he'd nagged
his mum all night to go on the
ghost train – then screamed to get off.
True, he'd fallen in the watersplash trying
to rescue his toffee apple, but that could
have happened to anyone.

"But Mum!" he begged. "All my friends
will be going."

"Bertie, I said no. No means no."

Dirty Bertie

Dad was in the garden raking the lawn.

"Dad!" cried Bertie, rushing outside.

"Bertie, I just swept that up."

"What?"

Dad groaned. "That pile of grass you've just trampled through."

"Oh, sorry." Bertie looked at his shoes. If people left piles of grass lying around how was he meant to avoid them?

"Dad," he said. "Can you take me to

the funfair tomorrow night?"

"No," said Dad.

"Why not?"

"I've got choir practice."

"But it's only on for one night."

"Sorry, Bertie. Ask your mum."

"I did. She won't take me either."

"Then you can't go."

"But … but … arghh!" Bertie stomped off, trailing grass all through the house.

Dirty Bertie

It wasn't fair. Why did he have such mean, selfish parents? They were always dragging him off to places he didn't want to go – like the dentist's or the countryside. But when it came to something important – like a funfair – they always said 'No'. Surely there was someone who could take him?

Of course! Gran! Gran was never too busy to do things with Bertie. She'd probably be grateful he asked her!

CHAPTER 2

DING DONG!

Gran opened the door.

"Oh, hello Bertie, come in. I was just talking about you!"

Gran was watching telly with her neighbour, Sherry. Bertie had met Sherry before. Generally he did his best to avoid her.

Dirty Bertie

"Hello Bertie! Come and give your Auntie Sherry a big kiss."

Bertie screwed up his face as Sherry planted a lipsticky kiss on his cheek. "Well!" she said. "Isn't he growing up fast?"

"I know," said Gran.

"Next thing you know he'll be coming round with his girlfriend!"

Bertie turned crimson. *Girlfriend?* He'd rather bring his pet tarantula!

Dirty Bertie

"Gran," he said. "Are you doing anything tomorrow night?"

"Tomorrow? No, I don't think so."

"Only I was thinking maybe you'd like to take me to the funfair."

"The funfair!" said Gran. "Goodness, it's ages since I went to one of those."

"I love a good funfair," said Sherry, helping herself to a slice of cake.

"So can you take me?" said Bertie. "Tomorrow night? Can you?"

"I don't see why not," said Gran. "Maybe Sherry would like to come, too?"

"What a good idea!" said Sherry. "We'll make a party of it. Won't that be fun, Bertie?"

"Oh … er yes," said Bertie. If he could go to the fair he'd put up with anyone – even Sherry.

CHAPTER 3

Saturday night arrived. The funfair was lit up like a Christmas tree. Bertie breathed in the sweet smell of candyfloss. Music boomed and thumped. The ghost train wailed. People on the rollercoaster screamed. *This is going to be brilliant,* thought Bertie. No mean parents to tell him what to do. He could hardly wait!

Dirty Bertie

They pushed their way through the crowds, looking at all the rides.

"Oooh," said Sherry, "I don't know where to start."

Bertie stopped. At one of the stalls was a sign in big red letters:

TRY YOUR LUCK! WIN A PRIZE!

His eyes lit up. In the middle of all the plastic watches and droopy dollies was the biggest jar of sweets he'd ever seen.

It was full to bursting with lollypops, toffees, chews and chocolates. Bertie reckoned there had to be at least a thousand sweets in there – enough to last him a whole week!

All you had to do was throw a hoop and land it over the jar.

Dirty Bertie

"Gran, can I have a go? Can I, please, can I?" Bertie begged.

"Of course, dear." Gran got out her purse and paid the Hoopla man. The best thing about Gran was she hardly ever said 'No'.

Bertie took careful aim. His first hoop fell way short. His second skimmed off the Hoopla man's head. His third hit the sweet jar with a plunk! and pinged off.

Dirty Bertie

"Oh, bad luck, Bertie!" said Sherry. "Let me have a try."

Gran and Sherry both tried their luck. Sherry won a prize – but not the jar of sweets Bertie had been hoping for. Instead she won two sets of Deely Boppers. Sherry put one on. They wobbled around on her head crazily, flashing red and green.

"You try them, Dotty," she giggled. "I bet they'd suit you."

Gran put on the other pair and they both doubled up, hooting with laughter.

"What do you think, Bertie?" they asked, posing arm in arm.

"Um, great," said Bertie. "But aren't you a bit, you know, old for them?"

"Ooh look! He's gone all pink!" giggled Sherry. "Are we embarrassing you, Bertie?"

Bertie trailed behind Gran and Sherry, watching their Deely Boppers bob up and down like yo-yos. This wasn't what he'd planned at all.

Dirty Bertie

In fact, he was starting to think this could turn into the worst night of his life. He seemed to be stuck with two alien grannies from the Planet Bonkers. What if someone from his class saw him? He'd never live it down.

Suddenly he stopped in his tracks. Climbing off the roundabout was a pale, smug-faced boy, holding a balloon. It was his sworn enemy, Know-All Nick.

Bertie looked around in desperation. He couldn't be seen with two mad grannies wearing disco lights. He had to escape!

Quickly, he grabbed Gran by the arm and steered her in the opposite direction.

"Where are we going now?" asked Sherry, hurrying after them.

"Look, bumper cars!" pointed Gran. "Bagsy I drive!"

Gran bought three tokens from the lady in the booth.

"Couldn't I go by myself?" pleaded Bertie.

"Don't be silly," scoffed Gran. "It's no fun on your own."

Gran dragged him over to a bright red bumper car and the three of them squashed in. He could see people pointing them out and laughing. He slid down in his seat, trying to hide.

Dirty Bertie

Dirty Bertie

The music started and Gran's foot slammed down on the pedal. The car lurched away.

BUMP! They crashed into the yellow car in front.

THUD! They swerved left and rammed a silver car.

"Ha ha! Got you!" yelled Gran. She wrenched the steering wheel round and they went into a spin before zipping off again.

"You're going the wrong way!" cried Bertie, pointing at the cars heading towards them like a swarm of bees.

"Rubbish!" said Gran. "They're going the wrong way."

BUMP! CRASH! WHAM!

A dozen bumper cars slammed into each other and shuddered to a halt.

Dirty Bertie

Arguments broke out as the drivers tried to reverse and thudded into each other. One of the attendants waded in to try and calm everyone down. Bertie meanwhile had spotted a boy with a balloon waiting with his dad. He sank even lower in his seat. It was Know-All Nick.

"Bertie!" said Gran. "What are you doing down there?"

CHAPTER 4

Bertie bit into a hot dog and tried to think. Somehow he had to get away from the grannies before they ran into Nick again. They passed a ride called Rattle and Roll. A sign in big letters said:

WARNING!

THIS RIDE NOT SUITABLE FOR UNDER 7'S,

OVER 70'S OR NERVOUS NINNIES.

Dirty Bertie

Bertie suddenly had a brilliant idea. All he had to do was pick all the scariest rides in the fair. Everyone knew grannies hated scary rides. They could go off and have a quiet cup of tea while Bertie enjoyed himself.

"What's next then, Bertie?" asked Gran.

"This one!" pointed Bertie.

"Heavens!" said Gran. "Rattle and Roll?"

Sherry looked up at the gigantic tower. "I dare you, Dotty," she said.

Gran's eyes twinkled. "I double dare you back," she said.

Bertie stared at them. "But … won't you be scared?" he asked.

"Of course we will," laughed Gran.

"I'll probably scream my head off," giggled Sherry.

"Me too," said Gran. "But Bertie can hold my hand."

Bertie took his seat between Gran and Sherry. The safety bar clunked into place.

GRUNT! SNORT! The machine sounded like a dragon. They began to rise slowly into the air. Higher and higher. Bertie tried not to look down.

"This isn't that scary," he said.

SNORT! WHOOSH! They shot

Dirty Bertie

earthwards at a million miles an hour.

Gran screamed. Sherry shrieked.

Bertie hung on for dear life.

UP they shot. Then DOWN.

UP. DOWN. DOWN. UP. DOWN.

Bertie clutched at his stomach.

Finally the ride stopped and the bar went up.

"Woo! That was amazing!" whooped Sherry, as they got off.

"I've come over all giddy!" gasped Gran. "Are you all right, Bertie? You've gone a bit pale."

"URRRRRR!" groaned Bertie.

They queued at one of the food kiosks. By the time they reached the front Bertie wasn't feeling quite so dizzy. He couldn't decide between candyfloss or a toffee apple or a fizzy drink – so he had all three.

Holding everything at once proved a bit tricky. He tried putting the candyfloss in his pocket to eat his toffee apple, but

Dirty Bertie

it got stuck to his trousers. When he pulled it off it somehow fell on the floor.

"Ugh! That's dirty, Bertie. You can't eat that!" said Gran.

"Why not?" said Bertie. "It's only a bit of grass." He picked off an ant and took a big mouthful. "Want shum?" he asked.

"Er, no thanks, you have it," said Gran.

Turning a corner, Bertie screeched to a halt. Know-All Nick had just arrived at the bottom of the helter skelter. Bertie looked around desperately for somewhere to hide. Any moment now Nick would spot them and come over.

He ducked under a barrier and joined a queue for one of the rides.

"Goodness!" said Gran. "Are you sure?"

"What?" said Bertie, looking up. He gulped. The sign said:

MIGHTY MEGAMAX
THE WORLD'S FASTEST ROLLERCOASTER.

Bertie had never been on a rollercoaster before. To tell the truth he wasn't sure he wanted to. But it was too late, they'd reached the front and Gran was paying for the tickets.

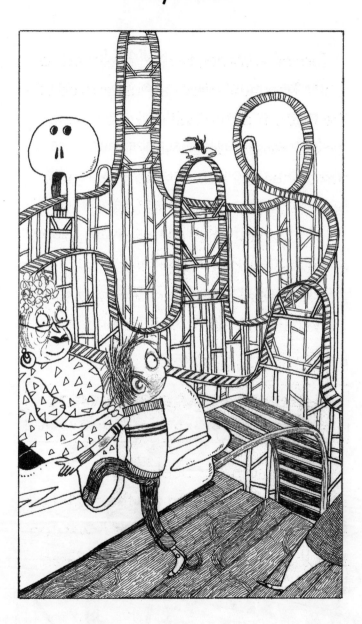

Dirty Bertie

RUMBLE, RUMBLE, RUMBLE!

Bertie clung to the safety bar as their carriage climbed the steep track. The rollercoaster looked scarier than Miss Boot on a Monday morning. When he glanced down his stomach gave a lurch.

Maybe all that candyfloss wasn't such a good idea. He felt sick. He felt dizzy. He wanted to get off.

Dirty Bertie

The carriage reached the crest of the hill and Bertie gaped at the drop below. ARRRRRRGGHHHHHHH!

They were hurtling towards the ground at the speed of light. He was going to die. They were all going to die.

"WHEEE!" whooped Gran and Sherry. "This is fun!"

Five terrifying minutes later the carriage slowed to a halt. Bertie staggered out. His hair stuck out like a hedgehog. His legs had turned to jelly. His face was a pale green.

Dirty Bertie

"Hello, Bertie!" jeered a voice. "Enjoy your ride?"

Know-All Nick was waiting by the barrier, and he was holding something large and shiny.

"Look what I won on the hoopla!" he boasted.

Bertie stared at the giant sweet jar stuffed with lollipops, chocolates and chews. His stomach heaved. He was going to be…

BLEUUUGHHHHH!

CHAPTER 1

"Don't you look smart!" beamed Mum.
"Come and look in the mirror."

Bertie plodded into the hall and
scowled at his reflection. He was
wearing a sailor suit. It was Victorian
History Day at school and everyone was
supposed to come in costume. Mum had
found the sailor suit in a charity shop.

Dirty Bertie

Bertie thought it was the drippiest thing he'd ever seen. The white trousers flapped above his ankles. The shirt had a stupid floppy collar. The hat had a wobbly blue pompom.

"There! What do you think?" asked Mum.

Bertie pulled a face. "I look like a girl," he said.

"Bertie, that's what boys used to wear in those days. I think you look very smart."

"Can't I go as a pirate? I've got the eyepatch and everything."

"It's Victorian Day," sighed Mum. "They didn't have pirates."

"A dustman then?" said Bertie.

"No!"

"Or a robber? I bet they had robbers."

"Bertie," said Mum. "I went to a lot of trouble to find you this costume and you're going to wear it. Now hurry up and get ready."

Bertie stomped up the stairs to look for his shoes. *It's not fair*, he thought. Why were parents always telling you what to wear? He didn't go round telling them what to wear!

Dirty Bertie

In his bedroom Bertie stared gloomily at himself in the wardrobe mirror. All his friends would have much better costumes than him. Donna was going as a flower girl and Eugene as a butler. Darren had said he was coming as a chimney sweep, which Bertie wished he'd thought of himself. All *he* had was a sailor suit with a stupid collar and a silly pompom. Maybe if he got rid of the collar the shirt wouldn't look so bad?

RIPPPP!

Uh oh – he seemed to have torn it.
Now the collar was hanging loose on
one side. His mum would have a fit if
she saw it. He yanked at the other side
to even it up.

RIPPPPPP!

Yikes!
That had
only made
things
worse. The
collar had

come off but the shirt had a big rip in it.
Now he looked like a scruffy old beggar.

Bertie stared. What a brilliant idea! He
could go as a beggar! In Victorian times
there were millions of beggars. You could
hardly walk down the street without
tripping over one. And he wouldn't even

have to change his costume. All it needed was a few small alterations. Now where did Mum keep the scissors?

"Bertie!" Mum shouted. "What are you doing up there? You're going to be late!"

"Coming!" said Bertie. He thumped downstairs and landed in the hall.

Mum stared in horror. "Bertie! What have you done?"

"It's my costume!" said Bertie. "I'm a beggar!"

Dirty Bertie

Bertie was still wearing his sailor suit,
or what was left of it. The sleeves hung
in tatters. The white trousers looked like
they'd been attacked by killer moths.
(Bertie had got a little carried away with
the scissors.) Bertie's feet were bare and
he was wearing a scruffy old cap on
his head.

Mum leaned heavily against the front
door. "How did this happen?" she
groaned.

"I did it myself," beamed Bertie.

"I can see that. You've completely
ruined your costume!"

Bertie shrugged. "Beggars don't wear
sailor suits," he said. "They have to look
poor. If they went round in sailor suits no
one would give them any money."

Mum peered at him closely.

Dirty Bertie

"What's that on your face?"

"Dirt," said Bertie.

"No, those red blotches. You look like you've got measles."

"Oh yes," said Bertie. "Poor people were always getting plagues and diseases, we did it in school. Don't worry it's only felt pen, it'll probably come off."

Dirty Bertie

Mum passed a hand over her eyes.

"Bertie, please! You can't go to school like that."

"Why not?" asked Bertie. "Miss Boot said to come as a Victorian, so I am. I'm coming as a beggar."

"But you look like a scarecrow."

"That's how beggars look," said Bertie. "No one said anything about having to be smart."

Mum looked at her watch. They were late already.

CHAPTER 2

The Victorian Day turned out to be a bit
of a disappointment. Bertie had been
hoping they might play some Victorian
games or try some Victorian sweets, but
Miss Boot had other ideas. To get into
the spirit of the day she had brought a
cane. She made them sit in rows and
practise their handwriting in silence.

Dirty Bertie

If anyone spoke or laughed or burped
they had to go and stand in the corner.
Bertie spent quite a lot of time in the
corner.

Dirty Bertie

After school Mum collected him and they stopped off at the supermarket. Bertie usually liked helping with the shopping. If he pushed the trolley and didn't bash into anyone, Mum let him have chocolate cake at the cafe. But today they had Whiffer with them.

"Sorry," said Mum. "He'll have to wait out here."

"Why?" asked Bertie.

Mum pointed at a sign by the door. It said 'NO DOGS ALLOWED' in big red letters.

Whiffer whined and wagged his tail at Bertie.

"I'll stay with him," said Bertie. "He gets lonely on his own."

Dirty Bertie

"All right," said Mum. "But don't go anywhere. And Bertie…"

"What?"

"Please take off that horrible hat."

Bertie took off his hat and sat down beside Whiffer. Whiffer rested his head in Bertie's lap and closed his eyes.

Shoppers passing by glanced down at the ragged, dirty-faced boy and his dog, sitting on the pavement. Some of them tutted to themselves while others shook their heads and gave him pitying looks. Bertie didn't notice people were staring – he was busy checking Whiffer's fur for fleas.

Dirty Bertie

Suddenly a woman bent down, smiled and dropped a fifty pence coin into his hat.

Bertie looked up in surprise. People didn't usually give him money. At least not total strangers. Did they think he was begging or something?

Dirty Bertie

He looked down at his ragged clothes and muddy shoes. Of course, he was still dressed as a beggar! The woman must have thought his hat was there to collect money! Bertie was thrilled. *This is fantastic!* he thought. *I bet Eugene doesn't get mistaken for a real butler!*

Wait till he told his friends about this tomorrow! His costume was even better than he thought.

Bertie tried out his sad face, waiting for someone else to pass by.

It worked. The next person, a man in a smart coat, dropped twenty pence into his hat. Fifty plus twenty that made um … seventy pence already! At this rate he would be rich – and all he had to do was sit on the pavement looking sorry for himself.

CHAPTER 3

For the next fifteen minutes, Bertie tried out different expressions on the shoppers passing by. Smiling, he found, was no use at all. It was better to look as if your pet earthworm had just died. Some shoppers hurried on past without paying any attention, but several stopped and soon Bertie's hat was filling up with shiny coins.

Dirty Bertie

He was just about to count what he'd earned, when a woman stopped in front of him. She was wearing a brown fur coat and a matching hat.

"You poor child," she tutted. "Where is your mother?"

"Oh, she's not here," stammered Bertie, putting on his sad face.

"You mean she's just left you by yourself? Is she coming back?"

Dirty Bertie

"Well … I expect so," said Bertie, glancing towards the supermarket.
"I expect she'll be back later." (He hoped it would be much later.)

"And does she know you are – begging?" asked the woman.

"Oh yes, it's okay, she doesn't mind," said Bertie. "She wants me to beg."

"Good heavens!" said the woman, sounding horrified. "Are you saying she forces you to do this?"

"Oh no, not forces me no, but if I don't do any begging we won't get any supper," said Bertie. "Cos my family are very, very poor. Poor as anything. My dad's actually a chimney sweep," he added by way of explanation.

The woman bent closer. She stared at the ugly red blotches on Bertie's face.

"You poor boy. How long have you been living like this? You don't look well at all," she murmured.

"I'm okay, really," said Bertie. "It's probably just a bit of plague or something."

The woman quickly took a step back. "You stay there," she said. "Stay there while I go and fetch someone."

Bertie waited till the woman had gone into the supermarket. He felt it would be wise to disappear before she came back. Whoever she had gone to fetch it could only lead to trouble. He picked up his hatful of coins. But, just at that moment, the woman reappeared from an exit to his left. She was followed by a tall security guard in a brown uniform.

Dirty Bertie

They were both marching towards him with a determined look. Bertie did the only thing he could think of. He fled. Jamming his hat on to his head, he darted into the supermarket with Whiffer at his heels.

"Hey!" cried the guard. "Come back!"

CHAPTER 4

Bertie looked around, desperate for somewhere to hide. People were staring at his ragged clothes and tutting at the sight of Whiffer. In his panic he'd forgotten that dogs weren't allowed in the supermarket. As he dithered, the guard appeared in the doorway and spotted him. "Hey!" he cried.

Dirty Bertie

Grabbing the nearest trolley, Bertie picked up Whiffer and plonked him in the basket. Then he set off at top speed, pushing the trolley in front of him.

"You! Wait! Come back!" cried the guard, chasing after him.

Bertie didn't stop to explain. He raced down the fruit aisle, scattering startled shoppers in his path. "Sorry! Sorry! Can't stop!" he panted.

A woman stepped out in front of him and froze with a pineapple in her hands.

At the last moment, Bertie swerved round her and skidded past the cheese counter. Glancing back, he caught sight of the guard puffing after him. He sped down the next aisle, narrowly missing a tower of toilet rolls. Whiffer was standing up in the trolley barking excitedly.

Dirty Bertie

Bertie looked up just in time to see a trolley parked across the aisle, blocking his way. The owner was reaching up to a shelf for a box of eggs. Her mouth fell open when she saw Bertie hurtling towards her. It was Mum.

Bertie tried to slam on the brakes, but the trolley didn't seem to have any.

Dirty Bertie

CRASH!

Whiffer went flying through the air
and landed in Mum's arms. Mum's
shopping went flying, too. A dozen eggs
hit the floor with a crunch, followed by a
pint of milk and a shower of cornflakes.

"Bertie!" cried Mum. "What on
earth…"

Dirty Bertie

Bertie was about to explain, when the security guard caught up with them. He stood panting for breath as the lady in the fur coat appeared, along with a small crowd keen to see what all the fuss was about. Mum sat in a pool of milk, staring at Bertie.

"Is this your son?" demanded the guard.

"I'm afraid so," said Mum, turning a little pink. "We'll pay for any damage."

"Never mind that," said the guard. "There's a law against it."

"You should be ashamed of yourself!" interrupted the lady.

"Me?" said Mum.

"Sending a boy of his age out on the streets to beg," said the lady. "I've a good mind to report you!"

"I'm sorry, I don't know what you're talking about," said Mum.

"Begging!" said the lady.

"Begging?" said Mum. She looked at Bertie. "Oh, I see! I'm afraid you've made a mistake. He's only dressed like that for school. He wasn't actually begging, were you, Bertie?"

There was an awkward silence as everyone looked at Bertie.

Dirty Bertie

He pulled off his hat, hoping he might look more sorry without it.

A shower of coins tumbled out and hit the floor, running in all directions.

"Um," said Bertie. "I can explain…"

BUM!

CHAPTER 1

Mum put down the phone. "Isn't that nice," she said. "Simon and Jenny have invited us all to go and stay next weekend."

Dad groaned. Suzy pulled a face. Bertie paused with a spoonful of soggy cereal halfway to his mouth.

"Who are Simon and Jenny?" he asked.

"You remember, they came to visit us at Easter – with baby Molly."

The cereal dropped off Bertie's spoon and splatted on the table.

"Not them?" he said.

"Yes, them – and please don't wipe that up with your sleeve."

"But I don't have to go, do I?"

"Well of course you do, Bertie. We're all invited. And Simon and Jenny are our friends."

"They're not my friends," said Bertie.

Dirty Bertie

"Well Jenny is my friend, I've known her since we were at school," said Mum. "Anyway, when people invite you to stay it's rude not to accept."

"It'll be boring. There'll be nothing for me to do!" grumbled Bertie.

"Of course there will. You can play with Molly. She likes you – remember?"

Bertie wasn't likely to forget. Molly was Simon and Jenny's little girl – a podgy baby with a mass of golden curls. She had stuck to Bertie like glue all day, crying whenever he went out of the room.

She had sat on his lap and pulled his hair. She'd poked him in the eye and wanted to kiss him.

Suzy looked up from her homework.

"Mum, you know I'm at Nisha's next weekend? We're going riding."

"I know," said Mum. "So it'll just be the three of us."

Bertie's sister grinned and stuck out her tongue at him.

Bertie was speechless. "That's not FAIR! Why does she get out of it when I have to go?"

"Because Suzy is busy. It's been arranged for weeks."

"I'm busy, too!"

"You're not, Bertie."

"I might be. I might be doing something important."

"Like what?"

"Well, like…" Bertie looked around for inspiration. "…Like staying here to look after Whiffer. Someone's got to."

"I don't mind doing it," offered Dad.

"I thought of it first!" said Bertie.

"Gran will take care of Whiffer," said Mum. "We are spending the weekend with Simon and Jenny. And Bertie, I will expect you to be on your best behaviour."

Bertie slumped back in his chair, miserably. A whole weekend of Soppy Simon, Drippy Jenny and baby Molly. He dropped his spoon in his bowl and watched it sink beneath a sea of brown goo.

CHAPTER 2

DING DONG! Simon and Jenny threw open the door. "Come in!" they cried. Jenny had Molly in her arms. "Look Molly," she cooed. "Who's this come to see you? Who's this?"

"Bee bee! Da da da!" cried Molly, reaching out her chubby little arms.

"That's right, it's Bertie! Clever girl!"

nodded Jenny, beaming. "Show Bertie what you can do!"

Jenny set Molly down on the floor. Last time Bertie had seen her she had been crawling around on all fours. Now she tottered down the hall on her dumpy little legs, looking back to check they were watching.

"Walking? Goodness! Aren't you clever, Molly?" said Mum, clapping her hands.

Dirty Bertie

"Isn't it amazing?" said Jenny, beaming with pride.

"Amazing!" nodded Simon.

Mum gave Dad a dig in the ribs.

"Oh yes, great," said Dad. "How long has she been – you know – walking?"

"Three weeks, two days," replied Simon. "I was in the kitchen the day it happened. Molly was sitting just there by the fridge, playing with her bricks. The next thing I knew she'd pulled herself up and just started walking. Didn't you, poppet? Yes you did, clever girl!"

Bertie caught Dad's eye. Were they going to be listening to this baby stuff all weekend? All this fuss over walking a few steps! Bertie walked miles to school and back every day and no one even seemed to notice!

Dirty Bertie

Molly had toddled into the lounge and came back clutching a small blue teddy. She held it out to Bertie, practically pushing it up his nose.

"Bee bee!" she said. "Da da da!"

"Oh, sweet! She wants you to have teddy!" said Jenny.

"Bertie have teddy? Bertie look after him?" asked Simon.

Bertie took the teddy. It had one chewed ear and its face was soggy with dribble.

Dirty Bertie

"Say thank you, Bertie," prompted Mum.

"Oh right. Thanks," said Bertie, holding the teddy as far away as possible. Molly toddled up to him and hugged him round the waist.

"Oh look!" said Mum. "She likes you, Bertie."

Molly tilted back her head and presented her lips. Her nose was runny.

"Molly want a kiss? Kiss for Bertie?" said Jenny.

There was no escape. Bertie bent down and allowed Molly to plant a big slobbery kiss on his mouth. It was worse than being licked by Whiffer. Molly giggled. She wanted to do it again. And again. And again.

It was going to be a long weekend.

Dirty Bertie

While the parents drank coffee, Molly dragged Bertie off to the playroom. He spent an hour making towers of building blocks so she could knock them down.

At five o'clock they gathered round the kitchen table to watch Molly having her supper. Jenny fed her spoonfuls of gloopy mush the colour of snot. Bertie thought it was hardly surprising that Molly spat most of it out.

"She's trying so hard," Jenny was saying. "Simon and I think she'll be talking any day now, don't we, sweetie?"

"Yes we do, sweetie," cooed Simon.

"Goodness," said Mum. "Bertie didn't start talking until he was almost two. How old is Molly now?"

Dirty Bertie

"Fourteen months," said Jenny. "It's still very young, but she's so advanced. Say 'Mum', Molly. Mum, mum, mum."

"Bee bee!" shouted Molly, banging her spoon. There was green mush all over her face and even a splodge in her hair. Bertie could hardly bear to look. And his parents thought *he* was messy!

Dirty Bertie

"Molly's little friend Nadia has just started talking," Jenny went on. "We see her at Teeny-Time Song Group on Fridays. But she's three weeks older and not half as clever as Molly, is she, poppet?"

Bertie yawned loudly. "When's supper?" he asked.

His mum glared at him. "Bertie, can't you find something to do?"

"What?" said Bertie.

"Do some colouring or something."

"I don't have anything to colour. Can I watch telly?"

"Anyway," Jenny went on. "Simon and

Dirty Bertie

I have this little bet on what her first word will be. Simon thinks it will be 'Dad'. But I know it's going to be 'Mum', isn't it, Molly? Mum, mum, mum."

"It could be 'Poo'," said Bertie, unexpectedly.

"Pardon?" said Jenny, faintly.

"Poo," repeated Bertie. "I was just saying, her first word – it could be 'Poo'."

"Bertie!" said Mum.

"What? I'm only saying! Babies poo all the time."

Jenny covered Molly's ears with her hands.

"Bertie," she said. "Why don't you go next door and see what's on television?"

CHAPTER 3

Bertie spent the night in Molly's room.
Her cot had been moved next door into
her parents' room to make way for him.
Bertie slept on an air bed with a Bunny
night light on top of the drawers beside
him. Molly's room was painted baby pink
with a border showing the letters of the
alphabet. A mobile hung from the ceiling

with fluffy smiling sheep. Bertie got
out of bed. If you wound up the
mobile it played a tinkly version of
'Baa Baa Black Sheep' and the
fluffy sheep went round and
round, bobbing up and
down gently. He stood
on a chair to wind it
up to see if he could
make the sheep go
round faster. The door
of the room creaked
open.

"BEE
BEE!" cried
a voice
behind
him.

Dirty Bertie

Bertie was so startled he took a step back and grabbed wildly at the mobile. For a second, his foot hovered in the air, then he fell back with the tangled sheep on top of him.

"BUM!" he said loudly.

Molly bent over him. She was wearing her pink bunny sleepsuit.

"BUM!" she said.

Bertie stared at her in horror.

Dirty Bertie

"What…?"

"Bum! Bum, bum, bum, bum…!" sang Molly, stamping her tiny feet. Bertie put a hand over her mouth to stop her.

"Shhh!" he whispered. "Naughty Molly. You mustn't say 'Bum'."

He took his hand away.

"Bum," repeated Molly, squashing Bertie's nose with her finger and giggling.

Dirty Bertie

Bertie went to the door and pushed it shut. If anyone came in, he was in major trouble. He tried to think. Babies simply copied whatever you said, so surely he could teach Molly something else? He knelt in front of her and gave her a serious look.

"Molly," he said. "Say 'Bertie'. 'Bertie'. Say 'Bertie', Molly."

"Bum," said Molly.

"No! No bums, okay? Look, what's this, Molly? What's this?"

He waved the tangled ball of sheep in front of her. "'Sheep', Molly. 'Sheep'."

Molly grabbed the sheep and dropped them on the floor. "Bum!" she giggled.

Bertie stared at her. This was a nightmare. If Simon and Jenny found out their daughter's first word was "Bum",

they'd have a fit. They'd probably pass
out. Mum would go bananas – and he
was bound to get the blame. It would
be no use trying to explain it was an
accident. Parents never believed you.
He'd probably have his pocket money
cancelled for a month. Or a year. Maybe
for the rest of his life.

He looked around the room in
desperation and grabbed a toy puppy.

"Look, Molly, doggie! What does doggie say? Woof! Woof!"

He made the puppy tickle her under the chin.

"BEE BEE!" said Molly, grabbing the puppy and kissing it on the nose.

"Yes!" nodded Bertie. "That's right. Bee bee! Bee bee!" It was going to be okay. Babies never remembered things for long. They said a word and then a minute later they had forgotten it.

Molly was toddling over to the door. It was shut. She pointed at it, wanting to get out.

"BUM!"

CHAPTER 4

Bertie was exhausted. He'd spent the entire morning playing with Molly. He'd played with her toy farm. He'd played Peepo behind the sofa. He'd watched *Fifi's Fairy Friends* six million times. Jenny said he was an angel. But the truth was he didn't dare let Molly out of his sight in case she said the unmentionable word.

Dirty Bertie

After lunch, Simon suggested they all take Molly to the children's playground at the park. Bertie was glad to get out of the house. He couldn't take much more of this. But if he could just manage to keep Molly busy for the afternoon, they could go home and he'd be off the hook.

Molly sat in one of the baby swings, but refused to let anyone except Bertie push her.

Mum, Dad, Simon and Jenny stood and watched.

A girl in a red coat ran over and sat on the swing next to Molly.

"Look, Molly, here's Nadia," said Jenny.

Nadia pointed to Molly. "Monny!" she said. "Monny!"

Dirty Bertie

Nadia's mum beamed proudly. "Clever girl! There's your friend, Molly."

She pushed Nadia on the swing. "She's picking up so many words now," she told Jenny. "There's no stopping her. The other day she looked at me and said 'Biscuit', clear as you like."

"Amazing," said Jenny.

"I know, and every day it's something new. How about Molly? Talking yet?"

Dirty Bertie

Jenny sighed. "Only baby words so far," she said. "But we don't want to rush her. This is her friend, Bertie, by the way. He's been a complete angel with Molly. Hasn't stopped playing with her all day."

Bertie hadn't been paying attention. Molly's swing had slowed down and almost stopped. She bounced up and down in her seat with frustration.

"BUM!" she cried.

Dirty Bertie

"Pardon, sweetie?" said Jenny.

"Bum!" sang Molly. "Bum, bum, BUM!"

"Oh dear!" said Nadia's mum, trying not to laugh.

"Bum!" cried Molly.

"Bum!" shouted Nadia, joining in.

"No darling, we don't say that," said Nadia's mum. "We say 'Bottom'."

She turned to Jenny. "Really! I thought you said she wasn't speaking!"

"She wasn't," said Jenny, turning pink.
"She's never said that before. I've no idea
where she could have learned it."

"Nor me," said Simon.

Mum looked at Bertie grimly. "Oh,
I think I can probably guess," she said.

Bertie decided it might be a good
time to slip away.

"Um, will you
excuse me?"
he said
politely. "I'm
just going for
a poo."